CHAPTER · 1 ·
Too Many Crimes go Unsolved

Green Janine woke up one morning and said to herself, "Today I am going to be a detective. I will detect crimes and trap robbers and burglars and all before tea time."

Just then the dog walked in.

"Are you any good at sniffing things out?" she said.

"What are you talking about?"

"I'm going to be a detective and you can help me."

"How is that going to work?" asked the dog very suspiciously.

"I want you to be my sniffer dog," said Green Janine.

"Oh no!" said the dog to itself.

2

"Yes - I can take you to the scene of the crime and you can follow the robbers' trail."

"You need a Bloodhound for that," said the dog. "In case you hadn't noticed, I'm not a Bloodhound. I'm not even one of those Springer Spaniels. I'm not an Alsatian or a Labrador. That's the sort of dog you want."

"I thought that you would be grateful - its just like going **WALKIES** - and you know how much you like that."

The dog's tail wagged before he could stop it.

"Good! Then that's settled," said Green Janine.

"We'll start straight after breakfast."

Green Janine went downstairs and said, "Today I am going to be a famous detective and detect crimes."

"That's nice," said her mother. "You'll want a good breakfast then because I understand detecting is a very demanding job."

"Right," said Green Janine, "and you'd better top up the dog's bowl as well. We're going to be a team."

"Look," said her mother "there's a story about a big robbery in the paper."

"Oh, that sounds interesting, doesn't it dog?" The dog nodded reluctantly.

"And," said her mother, "it's only just around the corner."

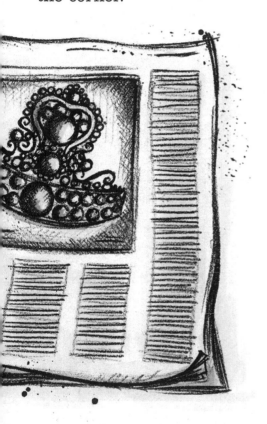

"Good, I wouldn't want to go too far on my first big job," said Green Janine.

"Have you seen the cat?"

"No I haven't," said her mother.

CHAPTER 2

"Hello, Hello, Hello..."

(I know the policeman doesn't actually say that but he should have done)

When Green Janine got to the gates of the big house where the robbery had taken place she found a very large policeman blocking her way.

"Yes miss – and what can we do for you?"

WE? thought Green Janine. She could only see one policeman, but then she thought the others must be hiding under cover in the bushes.

"I would like to go in so that I can sort out the answer to this crime."

"Oh, and by the way, just exactly what has happened here? My mother forgot to read the whole story."

"His lordship 'as 'ad burg-u-lars in the night," said the constable.

Hmm, that sounds nasty, thought Green Janine to herself.

"And the villains 'ave made off with her ladyship's favourite tiara," he said.

"Tarrara! Tarrara - what's a tarrara when it's at home?" said Green Janine.

"It's a kind of crown made out of gold and diamonds and the problem is, as I just said, it's not at home any more because it's been taken," said the policeman.

"Are you waiting for someone to bring it back then?" said Green Janine.

"No I'm waiting for the detectives to arrive."

"That's where I come in," said Green Janine. "I've brought my magnificating glass and this is my highly trained sniffer dog."

The policeman looked at the dog and sniffed.

"Well," he said, "I'm sorry but we can't go letting beginners trample all over the place — this is a job for the professionals."

"Just because I'm just starting out on my detecting career doesn't mean I'm no good," said Green Janine haughtily. "I'll have you know my teacher says I'm very good at investigations."

"Well, in that case I'll let you in," said the policeman "but you must promise not to get your fingerprints all over the place."

"I won't, I won't," said Green Janine. "I washed my hands before I came out."

Green Janine and the dog went into the big house and began to look for clues.

!?!?!?!

This was harder than Green Janine had first imagined and after half an hour they were still clueless.

"We're not getting very far very fast dog. I think you had better start sniffing a bit harder."

"It would help if you could tell me just what I'm supposed to be sniffing for," said the dog, who by now was getting a bit fed up with being a detective dog.

A short while later, the dog barked and
said to Green Janine, "What about
this? Do you think this
could be a clue?"

"What is it?" said Green Janine.

"Well," said the dog, "it's a book called 'Burglary for Beginners'."

"Hmm," said Green Janine.

!?!?!?!

"Let's open it up and see what it says," said the dog.

Inside the book someone had written:

'This book belongs to Bill and Bob
the burg-u-lars. If lost
please return to 72
The High Street.'

"**HA–HA!!** This is a real clue," said Green Janine. "They must have dropped the book whilst they were making their get away."

"Get away!" said the dog who was really impressed with Green Janine's powers of deduction.

"No time to lose," said Green Janine. "Let's get over there in double quick time and arrest them."

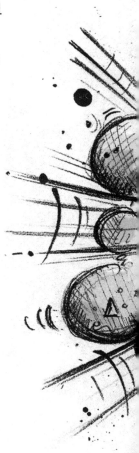

Just at that moment there was an

When the dust settled there stood
Mr Mephista!

"Hello," said Mr Mephista.

CHAPTER 3
Trouble with Transport

"**H**ello, hello, hello," said Green Janine. "Why did you say 'hello' three times?" asked Mr Mephista.

"Because we are helping the police in their enquiries and they always say it three times. And, I have to tell you, we have nearly solved the case of the stolen tarrara," said Green Janine.

"But what we need is transport with lights and neenaws to get us to the burglars' house."

"Done," said Mr Mephista and there was a BIG FLASH.

"You really aren't very good at this magic malarkey are you?" said Green Janine, a bit unkindly.

"What do you mean?" said Mr Mephista.

"This is an ambulance!" It's used for taking poorly people to the hostipal."

"You said flashing lights and neenaws," said Mr Mephista.

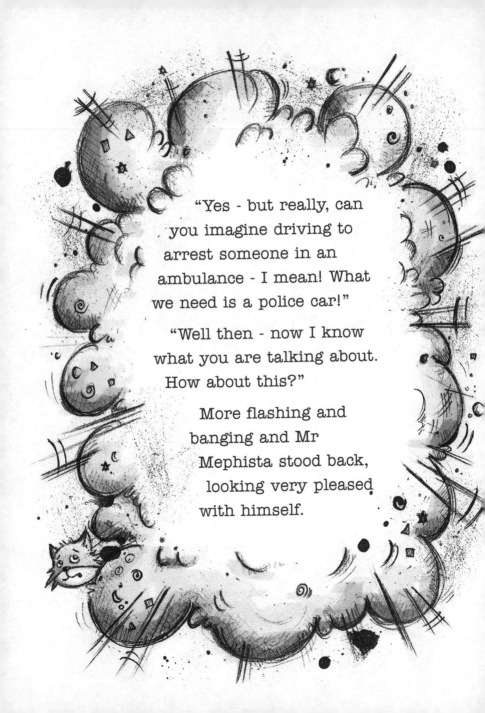

"Yes - but really, can you imagine driving to arrest someone in an ambulance - I mean! What we need is a police car!"

"Well then - now I know what you are talking about. How about this?"

More flashing and banging and Mr Mephista stood back, looking very pleased with himself.

A police car was standing there, all white with a big red stripe across the middle.

"That's absolutely super," said Green Janine. "But do you think we could have it outside on the drive rather than in here in the ballroom?"

"My pleasure,"
said Mr Mephista
and in another
flash they were
in the car and
ready to go.

"Problem!" said Green Janine.

"What's that?" said Mr Mephista.

"Well for one thing I can't drive and
for another the dog usually feels
sick when he's in a car."

"That's what magic is for," said Mr Mephista. Suddenly, the car was full of weird sounds and bright lights.

"Belt up," said Green Janine.

"I beg your pardon!!" said a very upset sounding Mr Mephista.

"What I mean is, fasten your seat belts please, it's what they say on television."

"Yes, well in my opinion some people watch too much television," said Mr Mephista.

"**NARR**," said Green Janine as the car roared off down the drive.

The policeman at the gate took his helmet
off and scratched his head as the car
flashed past. "Hmm," he said to himself,
"these police drivers are looking
younger every day."

It was just like magic.

Cars pulled in to the side of
the road to let them pass and a
lollipop lady held back a crowd of
children at the crossing. People
stood and gazed as the intrepid
detectives sped on their way.

"This is fun," said Green Janine, "in fact, this is great fun."

"A bit slower if you don't mind," said Mr Mephista. "I'd like to get there in one piece, and don't you think we should turn these things off now?"

"Why's that?" said Green Janine.

"I think we should approach the robbers' den silently," said Mr Mephista, "and then we can catch them unawares."

"Sounds like a good idea," said Green Janine. So they switched everything off.

The dog gave a sigh of relief and took its paws away from its ears.

CHAPTER 4:
The No-Plan Plan

They found the robbers' house and Green Janine drew up outside and parked. They all got out.

"What's the plan?" asked Mr Mephista

"Plan! What plan?" said Green Janine. "I haven't got a plan."

"You didn't have a clue either until I found it for you," said the dog.

"Just try to be helpful will you?" said Green Janine.

"Do you think they noticed us?" she asked Mr Mephista.

"Well, it's difficult to miss something as obvious as a police car parked outside your front door isn't it?" said Mr Mephista.

"I suppose so," said Green Janine. "But that's the answer, the direct approach. Come on we are going to knock on the front door."

"And then are we going to run away?" asked the dog.

"No!" said Green Janine. "We will identify the robbers and arrest them."

"How do you do that?" said the dog.

"I don't know, we'll just make it up as we go along," said Green Janine.

She went up the steps and rang the bell.

There was a moment's silence
and then the door opened slowly.

"Are you Bob or Bill?" said Green Janine.

"I'm Bob," said Bob.

"And is Bill as big as you?" said Green
Janine.

"No, Bill's bigger," said Bob.

"Much bigger?" said Green Janine.

"Twice as big!" said Bob.

"Hmm!" said Green Janine.

"Well, the long and short of it is, we have found your book and we have brought it back for you," said Green Janine.

"Which book is that?" said Bob.

"It's 'Burglary for Beginners' and you are under arrest!"

"You can't arrest me," said Bob.

"Why not?" said Green Janine.

"Because you're not a policeman," said Bob.

"I'm not even a policewoman! But I'm still going to arrest you," said Green Janine.

"Good stuff," said Mr Mephista.

"And you can be quiet too," said Bob who by now was getting a bit annoyed.

The dog growled.

"Look," said Bob, "I'm not going to be arrested so you will just have to come back tomorrow."

"I can't come back tomorrow, I have to go and buy some new shoes," said Green Janine.

"Well that's it then," said Bob. "Bye-bye."

At that point the dog sprang forward and grabbed hold of Bob by the leg.

Bob shook his leg vigorously but the dog held on.

At that moment Bill arrived and he **WAS** big.

"Oi!" said Bill, "tell your dog to let go."

"No!" said Green Janine, "and you are under arrest as well."

"Time for some magic," said Mr Mephista and in a flash Bill and Bob were in the bag. Well, each was in a bag of his own and judging by the noise they were making they were not too pleased about it.

"Now all we have to do is find the tarrara," said Green Janine.

"Not tarrara – it's tiara!" said the dog.

So they found the tiara and Green Janine tried it on for size.

"What do you think?" said Green Janine. "Not the sort of thing you could wear to school is it?"

"No," said the dog, "let's take it back to where it belongs."

Mr Mephista said he thought it was time for him to disappear.

So he did.

〰〰〰

Then they sent for the police to come and pick up the two unfortunate burglars in the bags.

"Take these burglars into custardly" said Green Janine.

"How did you get those two desperate criminals into those bags?" said one of the officers.

"Trade secret," said Green Janine.

The duchess was very pleased to have her favourite tiara back and she told the police superintendent that she thought Green Janine deserved a medal.

The dog sniffed loudly but the duchess said nothing about him.

She was obviously not a doggy sort of person.

The police superintendent asked Green Janine if he could have her telephone number so that he could ring her up if they got any more tough cases.

"Of course," said Green Janine. "Always glad to help the forces of law and order."

Then they were given a lift home in the police helicopter which had been sitting outside on the lawn.

"Indigo 99 to control," said the pilot. "We are now flying off to Green Janine's house. Estimated time of arrival 5 minutes before tea time. Indigo 99 out."

"Tango alpha tango alpha,"
said the man at control.

When they got there, the pilot put the helicopter down in the back garden and Green Janine's mother came out to see what all the noise was about.

"Well then," said her mother as they sat down for their tea, "have you had a nice day dear?"

"Yes thank you," said Green Janine. "Me and the dog solved a great mystery. We bagged the burglars and returned the duchess's favourite tarrara and everyone was very happy. Well, everyone except Bob and Bill the burglars that is. But I tell you what, being an ace detective doesn't half make you hungry."

"That's good," said her mother, "because we've got spaghetti on toast followed by an Eccles Cake."

GREEN JANINE'S RULES FOR COLOURING IN HER PICTURES

This is not a rule. This is how you can get free colouring pages. Just go to the Competition page at www.sevenarchespublishing.co.uk

1. Always colour me in green and colour my hair in a different green.

2. Always colour my dress in purple or mauve.

3. If you haven't got a purple you can make it by mixing red and blue.

4. If you are good at colouring don't go over the lines. If you are not good at colouring, or are little, you can go over the lines a lot.

5. When you have finished all the pictures, you could put them together to make a book and enter our FABULOUS COMPETITION. See page 56.

Just to let you know, I will not speak to anyone who colours my dress in PINK!!!!!!

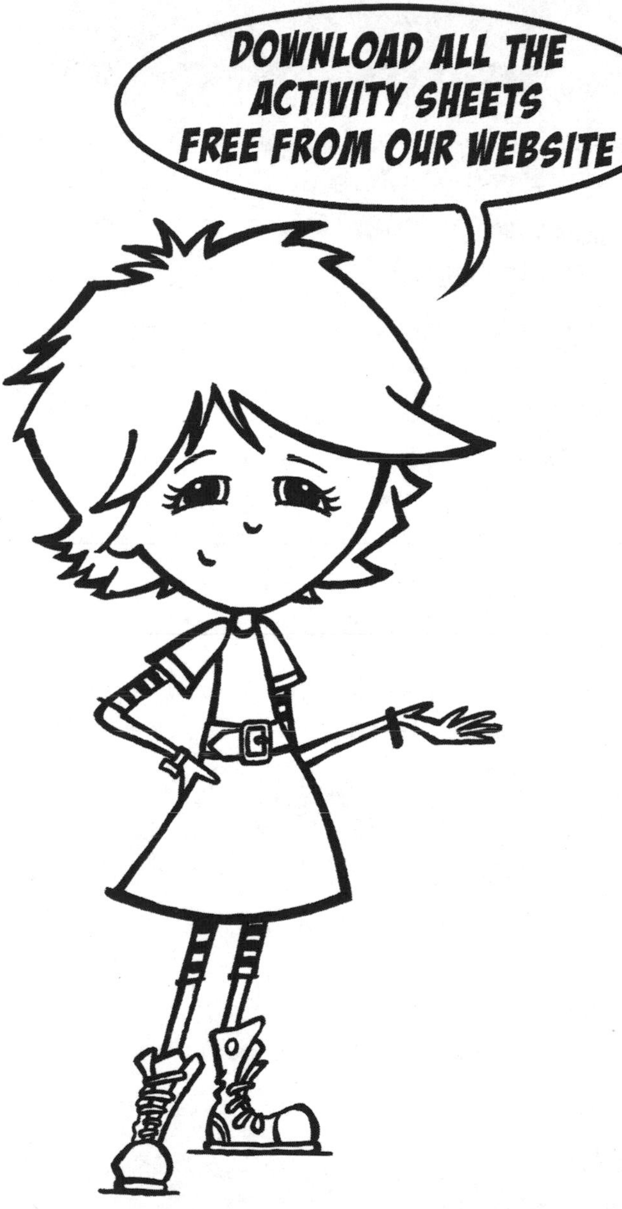
DOWNLOAD ALL THE ACTIVITY SHEETS FREE FROM OUR WEBSITE

FABULOUSLY FABULOUS COMPETITION

After you have downloaded the pictures from www.sevenarchespublishing.co.uk and coloured them in, you could make them into a book by stapling the pages together.

Books always have covers. If you design a FABULOUS cover for your book of coloured in pictures, you could win a prize in our book cover competition. Just take a photograph of your design for the cover, don't forget the title and the name of the author, that's you, and send the photograph to the email address: admin@sevenarchespublishing.co.uk

What's the prize? you ask. Twenty-five wonderful English pounds to spend on whatever you like!

Is there a closing date? No. Just check the website on the competition page and if you can see your cover there, you know we will be sending you your prize. We can't get it to you unless a responsible adult such as your parent, carer, teacher or librarian puts their address on the email. That way we can send them the money and they can give it to you.

HAVE A GO!

A LITTLE CAT PUZZLE

The cat wanted to be in the story but someone, I won't say who, cut out the cat's part, so the cat decided it would go its own way, as cat's always do.

If you look carefully you can see that the cat manages to squeeze into the story quite often. How many times does the cat get into the picture? Turn this page upside down to see if you were right.

A BIG WORD PUZZLE

Did you notice that Green Janine sometimes gets words muddled up? Well we all do sometimes, I suppose, especially if we are speaking a foreign language, but perhaps some people do more often than others. This puzzle is simple. Just find out how many words Green Janine gets wrong and then see if you can write them down on a piece of paper spelt correctly. Turn this page upside down to see if you were right about the number.

The policeman gets some words wrong as well, but that is a completely different matter, so don't include any words the policeman gets wrong.

Answer: There are eight cats.
The number of words Green Janine gets wrong is four.

ABOUT THE AUTHOR

Brian Tyrer was born during the Second World War. He lives in Lewes in Sussex. Green Janine Turns Detective is his first solo publication. In a former life he was a teacher and then a school inspector.

Whilst teaching, the staff from his school met with Alex Brychta, the well-known illustrator for Oxford Reading Tree and they described him. This is the drawing he made from their description. It's an uncanny resemblance.

ABOUT THE ILLUSTRATOR

John Bigwood says he studied Art and Design at
Bolton University and got a simply magnificent
degree. He doesn't look old enough for that, but he
must be because he is so good at drawing absolutely
everything. He lives in London in a flat with his
lovely girlfriend. His mum and dad live just round
the corner and make sure he catches trains on
time, and charges the battery in his mobile phone.
Even so it is hard to contact him because he leaves
it switched off almost always.

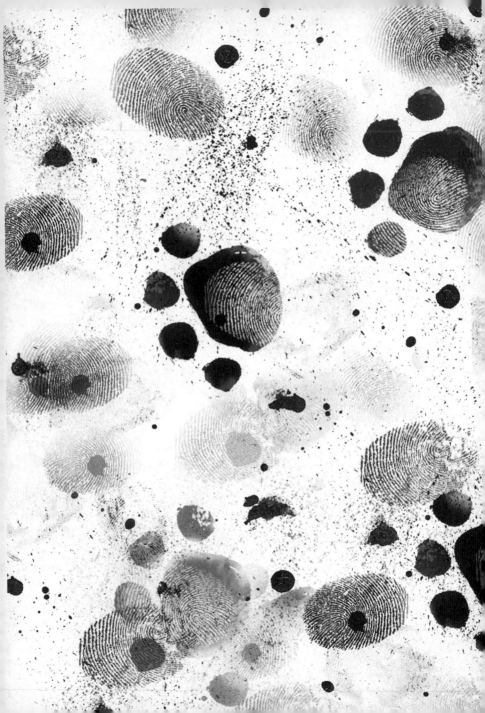